Timeless
Depths

ERICA VARELA

Erica Varela / Magesoul Publishing
PO BOX 580019
Bronx, NY 10458
www.magesoul.com

Publisher's Note: This is a work of fiction. Names, characters, places, and incidents are a product of the author's imagination. Locales and public names are sometimes used for atmospheric purposes. Any resemblance to actual people, living or dead, or to businesses, companies, events, institutions, or locales is completely coincidental.

Edited by **Soshinie A. Singh**
Cover artwork from **Shutterstock**

Bulk purchases from Magesoul Publishing are available with discounts.

Timeless Depths / Erica Varela -- 1st ed.
ISBN 978-0-9980403-2-5

DEDICATION

This book is for all the lovers who have love, loved and lost.

Remember to love, is to love oneself.

CONTENTS

THERE ARE NO RULES!

WE ALREADY KNOW TIME EXISTS, ITS
CLICKS BEGIN AND ITS TOCK A FINAL DEEP
WIDE BREATH.

WHAT WE NEED TO LEARN- IS TO LIVE,
TIMELESSLY.

<u>ERICA</u>

I am a house.
Inside a labyrinth.
Red brick walls
Cement sticks.
I know my way
I made the pattern exclusively.
Though to say; these patterns
I saw, I seen, and I've been present,
Sometimes to my fault of lost.

Made so rich, so crimson-
A hint of a noir soul.
A hint, unhinged.

Nevertheless, her naturally haunting beauty
remains.

When the day remained to be at its will,
Filled with strength.

Her wall –
        Collapsed.

FLAWLESSLY, FLAWLESS

Your face so perfect - fully painted.
Stokes blended so lightly
As the brush lightens all of your flaws.

A dusted canvas
Left in a corner,
You may never see again.
For these brown eyes will see,
The flaws you'd bring.

Still attached.

Flawlessly.

EL PRADO

I found paradise on your lips, on wooden
benches;
at the meadows.
Inside a silver ring engraved.

A memory we can't replace

Passed, velvet curtains and a snake vertebrae.

SMOKE EMBERS

I stood next to the wooden entry door,
You walked in.

I noticed, my mouth aphonic; voiceless.

I sat around the fire, as the ashes dried my
throat.

You walk on over to where I sit, in mid-
conversation; you spoke
with-out introduction.
Fixated by my eyes, you're all I see.

Words without ~~pause~~.

Weeks, since I last saw you.
Days confluence, our love you too's

Spoken whispers.

Take another gamble with me?
I'm intertwined in your speech.
Shot in the dark.

TILL THE END

With all due respect, I still love you.
Do you?
I chased you with words, at times
misunderstood.
You ran erasing the promises that could.
Astounded and bewilder.

SOMMELIER

In an endless embrace, my heart beats slowly-
faster
Thoughts of the world erase
With your breath of winter.
Touch made of velvet.
Your scent makes me tremble.
Awaken hidden comforts-
You're my drug that makes me numb,
From my soul to my fingertips,
Only you can make me cum,
With your wine stained lips.

Oxygen to suffocate.

Steer me anxious,
Caress me with soberness.
To our dark and endless place,
Weakening muscles.

Our eyes close; floating on dreams of a lucid
overdose.

AUDIO

What is the use in searching for answers, when you can just listen?

ROUTES

The time has come.
How I hate time-
There's no rewind, pause or fast forward.
The tics and toc's don't quiet down.
I don't even own a clock; But its sounds are loud
enough for my
Sensitive ears to hear.

                Can we be a painting?
                        Song?
                        Words?

When time ends, and it does,
Hands on clocks, with its loudest clicks,
Slowly become whispers for only our ears.

RIDDLES

Words written
Music our hidden messages
Late night talks
FaceTime.

A place we share.
Deep water mysteries.

RENEWAL IN VENICE

I remember that first time we kissed,
After that year, before our goodbyes,
Looked up to see your watery ocean eyes, fill
my veins.
I remember kissing your storm, falling from
your blue ocean heart.
I remember,
I remember us,
I remember it all!

What I remember the most?

My heart dying, in miss of yours,
We pulsate golden breath.

I remember all of this, for you are my treasure.
For a night.

Unsatisfied.

A BRAILLE GOODBYE

Your face ingrained in my memory
My heart is off limits and still.
You're making me sick!
You said you'd never leave,
Now we're strangers who have never met.
You are making me bilious.
Wishful thinking as I died in your bed.
After a night of revelry,
I walked away, never leaving a memory.

UN-NOTICED

Talk to me, you've recognized me before,
Just hear me out?

When I never left you on your knees,
All the times you needed me
Never have I left you invisible.

You said we could be friends.
What you hadn't spoken was,
On your time, your mistakes.

Urgency in weakness, demands.

Notice my cries.
Carry my crimes,
As I'm still carrying yours.

Unseen.

SWEETWATER

When did our love fade?
Was it at the bar?
Or when your eyes were laced on another?

You spoke: "you'll always be the one who broke me,
As a heart, puzzled like a jigsaw".

My answer: Do you pay attention?
I was standing there with a drink in my hand,
open voice and pierced skin.
As my semblance fell through,
When you didn't catch notice.
This water isn't so sweet as believed.
Unappetizing, really.

NOT YOUR FOOL. ANYMORE?

Share another lie with me dear, as you push me
away.
Keep me a secret,
And silent I will be
In your bed.

Speak with your lips
Your lies and crooked teeth.

Bright red face
Coarse hair.

Tell me this time, is not the time.

For your snowed in heart; no longer feels
Warmth.

What was *once, twice*, and by the *third* time, I
will disappear.

WHY ME?

This disguise has long lasted her years with me.
She'll never leave me.

    Mentally destroying everyone I love.

THE ONE IN QUESTION

I knew you felt lost,
I searched, and I found you.

I knew how it felt to bleed,
I covered your wounds.

I knew how it felt to feel lonely,
I stood by your side.

                I, unnamed.

I know many things
   "As well as"
I knew nothing of me.

EMOTIONAL ROULETTE

It was your hunger that killed me.
A starving sentiment,
Oh, what a lovely feeling.

One bullet, six chances,
first pull, kick back-

Metal bed,
Tagged casualty.

REALITY

I sit here waiting for the sun to exist once
again; to fake a smile.
Tell everyone I'm ok.
When the truth is, sitting on this cold porch at
4am,
I am drowning with the ocean that lays miles
away from my body, barely breathing; keeping
my nose above its waves.

I'm not manic, nor, am I depressed
 A "mixed state"

Smoking lungs, inhaling cancer,
Void filler.

My gift to you?
a clock.

                    Tic
                    Toc,
                    Tic
                    Toc.

Hands clicking,
Shows me we've come to our end.

I once did love you.
Never fully.
A stenciled shape,
Resembling a heart.

INSANITY

My mind the traveling carnival
A circus of thoughts
Open 365 days a year
Rain or shine.

PARAMOUR

It's laborious to write when you're happy
It's hard to spell.

Speak, for you see, I get tongue tied
Get a little scared, more frighten.

I spill out my words, through rough waters.

To feel you
Is all I want to do, in the morning
mid-day
Sinning nights,
Under the stars, above us.

On porches where strangers hear our sound,
when we become one.

KNOWN NAME

This race has become cumbersome
Extra body to replace,
Unwanted.

She lingers to walk into the unknown,
She'll follow us Page by page
Studies every line-

Burdensome.
Irksome.
Cessation.
Placeable.

Now?
     ~Weightless.

HARD FACTS

Trust.
Trust isn't easy for the invulnerable.

Trust is leaving me with slippery hands trying
to catch my heart; when I've always been afraid
of altitude.

UNEASE

If there's one thing about life, its living without fear.
Trepidation is **not** an option, unless you've concern movement.

BLUE BIRD STORIES

The blue bird said to the owl, it'll all work out,
we're going to be ok.

The owl replied *(nervously)*: I hope so.

Her response "I'm in love with you".

I promise, it'll be ok, stay hopeful.
I replied; I am in love with you too.

Their wings became messengers.

Direction?
Unknown.

TRUTH AND LIES

Do you always have an excuse before asked?
You're filling in the blanks here darling.

PSYCHOTHERAPY TALKS

Q: Show me what you're fighting for?

A: A breathless breath, suffocating lungs.

Q: Tell me who you're fighting for?

A: A known stranger.

CLOSED WINDOWS

Facing someone and saying your goodbyes
aren't the hardest.
It's what shows in their eyes.

Truth.

PATIENCE

Understanding the unknown is a privilege.
Forgiving mistakes, knowledge.

The wanting, the hope, Love?

Only we both know.
Or am I wrong?

For all I have is a heart of gold
With a balance of green
Tainted black.

Share your words with me.

OPEN INSECURITIES'

If I am (and will be) ever judged,
Make sure you observe my qualities

For I am a transparent book,
Always left closed.

MY PROMISE

This time I will keep my feet above ground.

For my body shouldn't move.

I found my void; that has last for so long in my
heart with the biggest hole, no one could ever
fulfill.

I run for safety, though my safety now is
You—

I can't promise to always be like the rest, but I
can promise; once I tell you, I love you-
It means,
I will love you forever.

A TROUBLED CURSE

Soil my home,
Skies to reach.
Re-charge this soul,
Re-wire my mind.

For when I rise-
I'll fall.

I will use these limbs
again.

Three times over,
Rising above,
Limitless skies.

TIMELINE KNOWN, 3 YEARS

This distance between, a vocal memory.
The silence you speak, so loud, in words-
You'll mute.

You flew far in our short time.

To where the skies touch the emotions of our
universe.
In separate lives.
Our parallels still speak
This distance, meets.

I sit and ponder where you'd be.
I lie awake,
wondering everything.

What meant you and I, there's no coincidence
as our stars, shined that March night.

Devine as she spoke, emotions overflowed.
  Embers to our rising fire.

Do you remember that time when we were quixotic dreamers?

CONFESSION

Non-fictional memories.
An Attached sentiment.

> We were
> Fervidly.

RECAPTURE

I deleted memories from my life.
I let them go forever, and the thought of them
never to be seen again; consumed my thoughts.

Not only did I set them free, I ignited my
memorization; fueling my emptiness.

GREY SKIN, BLUE BONES

Make-up and perfume to cover up this corpse.

VULNERABLE

I keep writing and writing as if tomorrow will
never come.
I continue to write, but, the true story has just
begun.
Southpaw writer, sheets left bare.

This skin, the canvas of my words.

GEMSTONES

For she, who brings love, also feels a pain for
the woman.
In as much as her agony, I will fall on my knees.
For without her treasures, I will remain a poor,
disease-ridden woman.

TO FEEL COMPLETE

There are people who poke holes in your heart,
and those who fill it.

THE POET

I'm not one to cry.
I'm not one to be put on a pedestal.
I am an imbalance sense of self.
Like an old time, clock that needs rewinding,
A doormat that's used to being walked on, now
weathered.
I am just the reflection you make me out to be.
But I am neither nor.
Like a fish who drowns in water,
A breath that forgets to breathe,
A facade of what defines make believe,
I am what you see in my false semblance.

I am my worst enemy.

TAKE NOTICE

I wanted for you to love me.
To speak of my name,
When I was too mute to call out for you.

SPILL ON ME

I've always admired writers, they who pour out
their hearts, before death.
I am an inkless pen, I write each letter with
blood stains.
Now, there's just blood across my fitted sheets,
where I lay in dried ink.

GREEN AND GOLD

They say when you wait patiently, that your
heart grows stronger.
How much truth in a false statement?
For you see, I've been waiting, and I don't
believe in time.
I'm sitting on a thread of this tethering line,
where there lies the unknowing.
I am waiting for when all my tickets, turn to
fines.
When they say waiting makes your heart grow
stronger.
Make sure she was worth waiting for.

RESIDENCE

This weather is insane!
Wish I could "come home"

(To the *ghost* of you)

ROYAL TURBULENCE

I'm her cash and she's my carter.

RAM

She's heartless, nowhere to be found.
Though, when she needs you, she's *always*
around.

LYRICAL

I'm blistered by the wind
You care about the sin.
My heart, of a joke, feels off to me,
It never sits.

STAY

A set of eyes.
Devour me whole and incomplete.

PATHWAYS

There're people all around us
You're next to me.
I'll look around, nothing will catch these brown
eyes-
As when the sun turns to the west and the
eastern darkness brings out the moon.
I'll leave and wander, where souls meet.
Observation.

TRAUMA

I want love.
I want all of it!
Every piece
Heart to heart
Glued strong together.

I fear that I am too damaged for your beautiful
soul.
I let my deceitful mind push a stray, for not; I
face the abandonment, again alone.

Reality?
I am the one who abandons myself.
For the fear that I am incapable of being loved.

ENDING DAYS

We fell asleep, drunkenly on our last night.
I held her so tight, no loosening of arms.
The next morning,
I awoke with your deadly words,
In a hurry, I rise up, melancholy.
As I bleed to hear you say, "Stay."

Wishing for your heart to speak-
You remained *silent*.

I, A COLOR BLUE

Blue, beautifully lays *black*
A colored emotion, felt.
My addiction must be worn.

Blue awaken me,
Tones are darkening.
Blue, my deep **blue**
How loving your peaceful darkness.

Blue, death–
Uninsured pain.
Crushed, cut and bleeding.

Blue, rebirth-—
Extinguish ~~hurt~~.
Lively, elated and frolicsome.

Deep waters, your beauty is captivating,
Times capsizing.
I've learned to breathe in your salty ocean
tides.

Blue am I breathing?
    with you?

STRINGS AND KEYS

There's a void in my heart,
I can't fill on my own.
There's a passion burning
So, must I go?

This time with feeling.

I can't suffice,
When on repeat.

Not knowing who I am?

The need is crippling, cracking.

Watch me go spineless,
Spreading long length wings.

For I am small.
Dare me to believe.

POSTULATE

How much hurt can a hopeful heart endure,
before she becomes numb?

—I believed.

Why couldn't you give a sense of reason?
I needed you to receive.
adumbrate.
Wooer.

It's been years,
I've been dreaming.
Giving up my soul
To keep your frigid feeling.
Though my dreaming,
Flows goldenly in these veins,
Now there's extinction to blame.

I'll follow through, erase your pain.

How could I hurt you?
You broke this heart, cryptic and unseen?

I lost myself in our creation, you set ajar.

Did you *trust*?
Did you *believe*?

Deemed and understood.

PAGAN GODDESS

Manifested you, I said.
Her hair a bleeding red--
Skin on lips, hearts' a pause,
Beating underneath
You.
Should I run?
Or shall I fall?
Before the dark and burning sun.
I saw before you, after there; none.
Your eyes binded a greenish blue, to blind me
from the lies,
That came before you.
This clumsy girl doesn't fall so easily.

A knee on the floor--

A SONG FOR US

Show me love, show me love, with your eyelids
closed
I want to feel your pain
Desires burning flame.

She caught the burn, but, the z's let her fall
asleep
I caught the burn and learned,
I'm in too deep.

She's got a hold on me
A hold of me
Am I alive?
Or have our lives gone black

I took her silence left it buried, 6 feet
underground
She took my pain, yet again; just to hear a
sound

Her muted silence on private grounds
To think she'll never be found,
next to the soil, that boils, it screams my name
I'm not soiled, or loyal
I've burnt, in her flames.

INTERTWINING SNAKES

Take me for granted,
I know your pleasures,
In the games you play.

Suck me into your charm,
Like the empty promises you've made.

Are you lonely now?
this time around.
isn't it bittersweet?
Chain-less cuffs.

I'm no longer your savior in need.

I won't fall!
empty promises made so sweet.
In the pleasures of your game-less piece
Selfish needs.

Your snake-skin moon wrapped around,
inflexible grip.
Sliver of your tongue --yearning for attention.

We're Everything we couldn't be.

Still intertwined.
Inexterminable.

THE SPARK THAT IGNITED OUR FLAME

"We" wooden matches.

Before, our spark ignited,
Our fire became flames.

Are we flammable?

This time let's begin, before our burn.

Strike a match.
We're still warm.

BLURRING THE LINES

I'll always remember you,
Despite our challenges
We always made it through.

"But"

This time our distance, not far.
Mental metal bars.

SAY WHAT YOU MEAN

All I wanted--
Your honesty.
Don't elaborate,
Hidden lies.

You know I understand you?

Not one to judge.
My heart is broken,
Can we repair?
Hearts who need.

THE BIRD WHO LIVES ON BUSH ST.

Keep those wings,
Continue on this movement.

Come fly with me?

Without restriction.

NON-FINISHED START

A start that kept us breathless.
An end to cause a shake.

Once again here,
Breathing.
With you.

NEW YEAR'S EVE 2018

Busy night you said,
I might not make it.

I stay in for you, in the cave of my room; it's not
the same without you.

You arrive.
I'm here—
Hour 11:40pm.

We go outside, precious sad eyes,
I keep you near.
Holding you, kissing you,
Fully and whole heartedly.

We smoke as chimneys.
Us both,
    Unforgettable memory.

A SHORT STORY "HOW WE BEGAN"

Unknown?
Decided.

Will I go?
I feel anxious, a bit of nausea.
Firm pulls
Powerful push,
Heightening my senses.

Turn the key.
Car packed street.
Around this corner, open space;
Stow.

Night still young,
My arrival, neither late.
Nights a young,
In an age.
I'm invisible
And *mute*.

Magnetic perception, powerful and keen.
Exquisite timing--

Both our eyes,
Laced moreover rivet.

Blue velvet sleeves,
You quietly move, next to me.

March air congeal breeze
Hot sweats sizzling, flourishing palm trees;
Seeds breed green.

Night near end.
I'm asked to stay;
You're asked to stay.

Both separately.

A bed made for one.
Both bodies share.

Blankets not enough–

Her heating.

On top of her body,
Lips to lips.
Furthermore.
Tangled snakes.

Morning, too quick for rising,
Our moon still visible—
On rooftops, our voice mute less,
Filling our lungs with the flames of night.

To leave -- such difficulty.
You ask to walk with me.
Moving our feet together; as we skip lines and
beats.

Stop at the corner!
With-out movement.

Closer steps; stop for touch.

A kiss goodbye,
To last another thirty-minutes.

Apart we walk,
Both, turn-around,
Exhibit for display.

Place key in ignition.

"Ding"
A text: When can I see you again?
Reply: tomorrow night?
Response: Yes please.

Our words limitless.

My heart?
A mountain cliff.

Your hills?
A fall for concern.

Fearless heights.

SUFFICIENT THOUGHTS

I know this feeling,
Been here before.
Confusing emotions,
Overflow.

With days turned to months now years.

Tumultuous thoughts,
Racing with words; through my mind,
Only my brain can raucous.

Am I blinded?
Cover my eyes in transparency.

Rough and strident.
Mutually harmonious.

Unrestrained.

PRISONER

These walls have become my prison, the smell
of smoke in my room, stale, stealing oxygen
from my lungs.

I cannot breathe.

Crying out in tears so dry, my face now peeling.
Feel my pain?
Hurt?

Unnamed.

I am slipping.
I am Hurting,
Am I dying?

Your love and your lies both smothering,
Unnoticed moments.

Open your eyes!
There you'll find me.

MY FIRST DEATH

I died in childhood.
Rewinding, as an old memory.

This is my life every day.

Realizing that I've never fully lived.

Then I realize, again?
It's not my craziness that has me here, still.

Valuable soil keeps piling onto my filthy bones.

In this grave I have shared with you!

MEETING SOULS

In this lifetime, I have met; so many deadly
souls,
That I no longer know, who is and isn't
breathing.

Am I what I write?

I have never been introduced to my own being.
In search for myself.

SHE IS NOT ME

Her tears, such a god-damn beauty,
Falling from her cheeks.
A gorgeous red face filled in anger;
Showing she cares.
She'll bleed ripping out her insides.

To see you go.

THREE CLAPS

Let's play?

1.
2.
3.

Find me.

I PLEA THE 5TH

I am just your beautiful liar.
Believe me.

EMOTIONAL RISK

You can Love!

Don't be scared.
(there's always a door)

PAPER THIN

Fulfillment?

Have you ever felt hungry?
--I am starving.

Satisfactions' never felt.

FALSELY ADORED

Is this true?
Speak my skies of blue?

Is this an *illusion*?
Reverie.

My heart replies: hasn't it always been?
Fictitious.

Mind games for one.

WOODEN BARN DOOR

Slowly you shut your room's door
For a night and a day.

Downstairs he sleeps, quietly.

Unclothed and nude we lay in your bed
Making love, hours long.
Moans so loud for an awakening.

He wakes up.

Closing the front door, as he leaves.

Louder and louder we get,
Moving passionately in soft bedsheets.

Louder and louder you moan,
 My lips soaking wet.

DISTINGUISH

It's all I know,
All I remember.

Been falling–
Recognize?

Hands ~~without~~ catch.

RUNNING FOR CHASE

Irrational steps,
Running to an old paradise,
You left long ago—
Emotionally dissatisfied.

Chasing after embers, heating your heart
While blistering in my tropical lush.

To feel alive once more.
Conscious and awake,
Chase me forward.

ATTENTIVE

Spell out your words for me,
Understandably.

I listen, wide open ears–
Noise spoken through lips.

Mindful learning.
Magnanimous.

LOVE IN THE DARK

I'm still in wait for your arrival.

I won't remain stagnant,
For you.

Holding onto hope, you'll soon vision.

My grip is starting to slip,
Time is passing,
With your heart–
A miss.

HEART THIEF

An endless thought; you remain in my head.
                    Heart.

No matter the lover, I still can feel you.

You're my absent intricacy—
mislaid.

SEWN PAGE

I wrote you a note from a ripped-out page, I tore
a piece, words in ink.

My journal smells of me—

Am I still in your wallet?
A scent unforgettable.

Hidden and folded,
Memory.

DEEP BLUE SUBMARINE

You've rotated me and left me spinning,
abstain at least.

Yearning.

WE BOTH KNOW HOW A WOMAN WITH SHORT WORDS CAN BE

I gave you my heart, before I handed you the
key.
Being unlocked–
You turned the key.

Lost entry,
From pockets to drawers.

Can you send it to me?

TRANSITION

Wonders only lead you to a life of non-fulfillment.

SOUNDS SO DELICATE

Everyone; becomes someone else,
if not for you, I'd be with you.

you're like an assault upon my circled heart,
I can't be myself and someone else too!

these simple things matter and mean to me--
as I cared for everyone,
No one cared for me.

A LETTER

Dear Us,

We're not done yet.

Sincerely yours,
~Meadow

BIRDS AND FEATHERS

I found myself again, as if a new finding.
I'll hide in the shadows,
To understand a light,
Hidden in me.

Three years trapped–
Clipped wings.
In unlocked cages.

Am I worth it?
I? strong enough?
Keep still, these steps shake,
This time I won't break.

I'll fly!

Giving up is not a choice.
Still in fright,
I'll take that risk in your darkest hour.

Find return in my own power,
Catapult like a boomerang–
To return.

MATCHBOX

One strike across 200 wooden matches?

You and I--
Cause flames.

DID YOU READ?

I write to you as my only love;
I wrote to you, completely different.
I've written to tell you, you hold this heart of
mine.

More than anyone has ever done.

~it was you.

WATER TWO DROWN

I tried.
I really did this time.
As the warmth ran across my body; through
my veins, onto outer skin.

Swam your salty life like sea, in depths so deep,
mistaken for oxygen.

YOU'RE ABOUT TO JUDGE

Childhood innocence.
wise youth.
Ripe and raw; my maturity.

I've suffocated in dry dirt–
Multiple times.
Felt; how to live without breath,
drowning in breathless waves.
Burning inside; spilling over my olive skin,
And set ablaze.

How hard to fly with no wings?
For I am a bird.

I've learned on my own.

Try if you must.

Define me?

FIGHTING FEELINGS

I hope you'll remember the way I held you,
Arms wrapped tightly and gentle
For your safety, to feel free.

Am I as forgettable?
You felt as believed.

Your eyes; shy a green,
Giving away.

I sense, where your heart was--

Is.

<u>LEARN ME</u>

Invisible.
I promise, take a look closer.
Whisper.
Listen to this silent heart.

Think of me–
I'm shown transparent.

Listen.
With your ears for the frequency's and cosmic
words,
for you to hear.

Remain quiet—

BLACK AND WHITE

Bittersweet.
Taste our tongues?

Your memories are with me.

As an epitaph written in
Silent movies.

Vocal noises heard.

Both–
Two hear a sound.

THIS DAY YEARLY

Last year, you couldn't make it.

This year, once again, unseen.

– I wanted you last year.

This year—
The same.

As years fell behind birthdays before.

DAY SIX

Exultant - sky high.
Colors–

Fear.
Euphoria.
Irritated.

> *"Entering my true self".*

I worry.
My universe in bed.
what to do?
She's rarely depressed (~~she's not?~~) Does she
need help--

From a manic depressive?

FOOLS

Why do we allow ourselves to fall in love?
We both know, how it ends.

Or do we?

NEVER ENDING

How sweet the smell of a lifeless soul–
'Tis shall be I.

Though how much more delightful to feel
death?
(Un)completed skeletons.

You & I.

THE UNNAMED, NAMED

We had love in its rarest form
"Stay," you said,
Believe me when I say it's you and I
And patiently I'll wait for your return.

Three letter name and Irish decent
Ali, in all you've said,
Was I your paradise?

Or something said.

Give me truth in validation.

A Scorpio's sting, rising pain
In the unknown depths
As an hour glass has its sands, untimed.

Let's rewind.

I needed you, how could you not see the tides
drowning me lifeless

Was I not an importance?

STRANDED SHIP

I see your eyes in the ocean, lakes and seas
Like an abandoned ship, looking for its tow
Left alone floating
Waiting on survival

That survival I'm afraid,
Is you.

SOME HELP HERE

This confusion of a feeling you want me.
You miss and need me
Us

Could I trust your eyes again.

HEAT

Whom have you become?
You and I live for our secrets
And now you can't contain to stay-
Since the morning sun.

Tell me once more, how you loved me.

TALENT

If I knew before my face smacked your cement
wall
I could tell you, I wouldn't have stayed.

But once again, my head left my heart
And I ate up all your words in hunger,
As a disappearing act,
Where did you go?
Flashing bye.

Illusionist.

WOMAN

This girl doesn't need your I love you.
THIS woman needs to be shown words.

Action.

Tell me when you're ready to notice me.

LIGHT

Can we just take a break?
Come out,
Say it.

It's getting cold without sun's light.

...and everyone knows

HARP

Today we'll spend in bed
Lights on
Covers off

You and I.

Our songs are my favorite.

Baby, I unlocked your cage the first time we
met,
How else would you fly?

SYRUP

Morning pancakes were my favorite with you
Walking blocks, hand to hand
With a kiss on every corner.

Mornings with you.

CONVERSATIONS

You love me.
You need me.
You miss me.

Your mind makes nonsense,
When your delivery hasn't made it home.

~Still.

ERICA VARELA

HOLD THE WARMTH

When we meet, and the fumes settle
Would you have a match?

TIMELESS DEPTHS

You and I have no ending.

THINKING OF ME?

I know your face, so well
Your structure, smile, eyes, scent

I feel your soul beginning to cradle
In your darkness at dawn
Its threshold a sinkhole.

And still I wake alone in sheets.
Reminder, of your quiet thoughts

Keepsake.

I'm sorry.

(sometimes)

MADNESS

I kept silent for so long
My breath deflates oxygen
Suffocating blacken lungs.
I stayed along with your feet,
A chance for truth

Let the memories go.

Realizing love, without return
Rewinding time.
Irrational incidents
Where I became lost for some time.

To fade away
Would I have to let her heart go?
Or release mine?

I just want you back in my arms
To keep you safe.
Like you were never mine.

Cache.

STEEL WALLS

I gave you all of me,
So, I thought.
Opened my fragile heart, just for you.

Was that enough?
What more do you want from me?

Everything I did in your eyes
Came out, dissatisfactory.

Beaches kept
Scars that never fade.

I bled for you
For months!
Always to be reminded of you.

I promised to never let you go...

As you did.

You and I, simply unlockable.

ABOUT THE AUTHOR

Erica Varela was born and raised in Perth Amboy, NJ. She currently resides in Los Angeles, Ca. In addition to writing, she enjoys a staff position with one of the most successful music record labels in the world, WMG. Staying true to her passion for writing as well as music. She is accredited for co-producing and composing music for LA's Underground music scene, and has fronted many bands, including her own.

As in any natural progression, she is now ready to pursue her next adventure and love, Poetry.

CONNECT WITH THE AUTHOR

Erica Varela

Website: ericavarela.com
Instagram: writerericavarela
Facebook: Erica Varela (@writerericavarela)

OTHER BOOKS BY:
ERICA VARELA

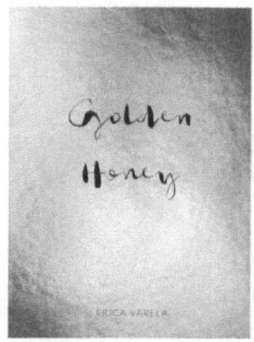

Golden Honey   Set Free

Available on all
Online bookstores

AVAILABLE

Magesoul Publishing is now accepting submissions from writers in the future who wish to get their book published through this corporation.

Submit or send inquiries to:
submissions@magesoulpublishing.com

www.ingramcontent.com/pod-product-compliance
Lightning Source LLC
Chambersburg PA
CBHW052001170626
46808CB00007B/2723